Text © 1986 Catharine Gardam
Illustrations © 1990 Gavin Rowe
All rights reserved
First published in Great Britain 1990 by
Julia MacRae Books
A division of Walker Books Ltd
87 Vauxhall Walk
London SE11 5HJ

British Library Cataloguing in Publication Data

Gardam, Catharine
The animals' Christmas
I. Title II. Gavin Rowe
823′.914[J]

ISBN 0-86203-432-9

Printed and bound in Hong Kong by
South China Printing Co. (1988) Ltd.

The Animals' Christmas

Catharine Gardam

with pictures by
Gavin Rowe

Julia MacRae Books

A DIVISION OF WALKER BOOKS

High on a hill stood a ruined abbey church.
At the foot of the hill was an elegant village
church.
Half way up the hill was Hawthorn Farm,
where Sam lived with his mum, his dad,
and his two sisters, Jane and Lucy.

It was Christmas Eve and the children gathered
holly, ivy, and mistletoe.

Sam and his dad went into the wood
behind the farm and chopped down an
enormous Christmas tree. They carried it
down the hill to the village church below.
Two bushes on legs followed behind.

The church was full of
busy people, and soon
Dad and the children
were busy too.

When they had finished, Sam, Dad, Jane and Lucy
set off up the hill. Far above them, Mum stood
at the farm gate. She was shouting and
waving and very pink in the face.

"I wonder what's up?" said Dad.

"Oh! Oh!" cried Mum,
"the hens have gone, and
all the baby chickens!"
"What?" roared Dad.
"And Buster the cockerel! I
can't find him anywhere."
"We must all hunt in
the fields," said Dad, and
he whistled for his sheep
dogs to come and help.
No dogs appeared.
"Bess! Floss!" Dad yelled
in a fury.
But the dogs were
nowhere to be found.
Sam looked into the cow
   byre. It was empty.

"Dad! Dad! The cows have gone!"
"And the pigs," cried Lucy,
peeping into the sty.
"And Binks," said Jane.
"Binks the bull is not in
his byre."
They ran round the farm
looking for the animals.
Nellie and Harold, the two
fat geese, were missing. So
was Marigold the turkey.
All the sheep and both the
rams were gone from the
hayfield. Even Jackson the
cat and her three little
kittens were not by the fire
as usual.

"Call the police!" bellowed Dad, and he tore his hair.

Mum rushed to the telephone.

By the time the policeman came panting
up the hill, it was snowing very hard. He
helped the family hunt through the fields,
but it was getting darker and darker and
colder and colder, and there was no sign
of the animals.

Down the hill, through the
dark night and swirling snow,
the windows of the village church
glowed with candlelight.
The bells began to ring, calling
everyone to church to celebrate
Christmas.
"Now then," said Mum, "we are
all going to church."

"No, we are not!" shouted Dad. "We
must keep looking for the animals."
"You are coming to church with the rest of
us," said Mum in a quiet, determined voice.
"I'll come too," said the policeman, and
he and Mum marched Dad and the
children down through the thick
snow to the little path which
led to the church.

When they arrived, the service had already begun.
The candles shone brightly and everybody sang:
"Hark the herald angels sing,
Glory to the newborn King . . ."

Soon Dad was enjoying himself so much that he
stopped fretting about the animals, and sang and sang:
"Peace on earth, and mercy mild,
God and sinners reconciled."

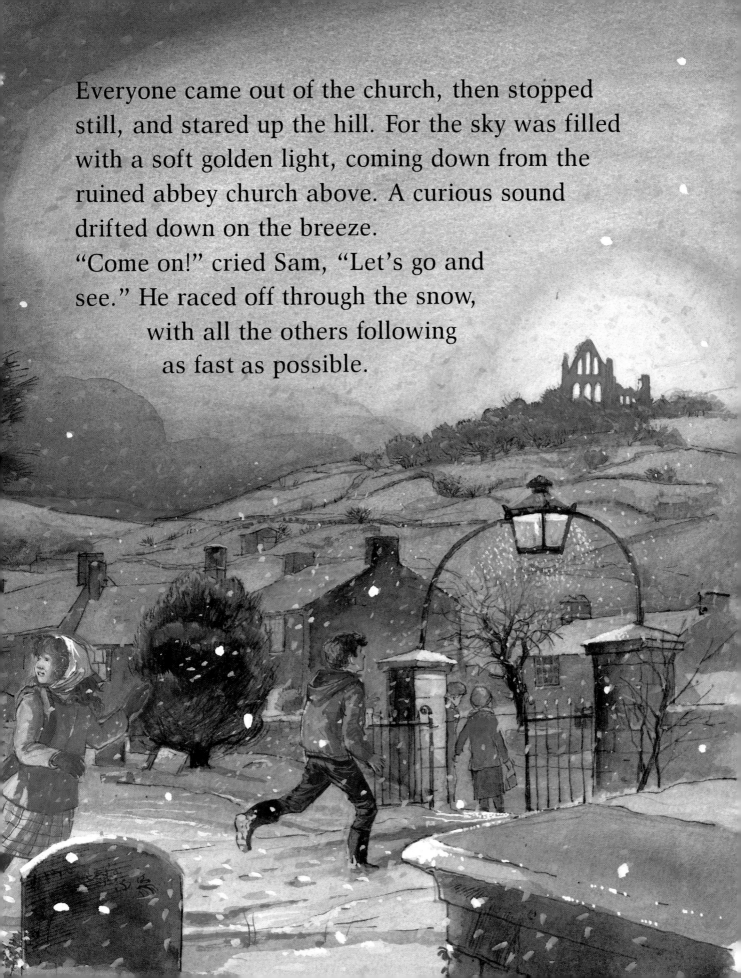

Everyone came out of the church, then stopped still, and stared up the hill. For the sky was filled with a soft golden light, coming down from the ruined abbey church above. A curious sound drifted down on the breeze.

"Come on!" cried Sam, "Let's go and see." He raced off through the snow, with all the others following as fast as possible.

As they climbed nearer the abbey, the sound became
louder and louder. It was a strange sort of singing,
and when Sam peeped through the old broken
doorway he saw the strange singers.
For there were all the animals, singing with the angels.

And soon everyone
shared in the animals'
Christmas.
"Hark, the herald
angels sing,
Glory to the
newborn King!"